★ WE ARE HEROES ★

RACE FOR HOME

by Jon Mikkelsen
illustrated by Nathan Lueth

Librarian Reviewer
Marci Peschke
Librarian, Dallas Independent School District
MA Education Reading Specialist, Stephen F. Austin State University
Learning Resources Endorsement, Texas Women's University

Reading Consultant
Elizabeth Stedem
Educator/Consultant, Colorado Springs, CO
MA in Elementary Education, University of Denver, CO

STONE ARCH BOOKS
www.stonearchbooks.com

Keystone Books are published by Stone Arch Books
151 Good Counsel Drive, P.O. Box 669
Mankato, Minnesota 56002
www.stonearchbooks.com

Library of Congress Cataloging-in-Publication Data
Mikkelsen, Jon.
    Race for Home / by Jon Mikkelsen; illustrated by Nathan Lueth.
    p. cm. — (Keystone Books. Everyday Heroes)
    ISBN 978-1-4342-0786-9 (library binding)
    ISBN 978-1-4342-0882-8 (pbk.)
    [1. Bicycles and bicycling—Fiction. 2. Homeless persons—Fiction.]
I. Lueth, Nathan, ill. II. Title.
PZ7.M59268 Rac
[Fic]—dc22   2008008120

Summary: Tomas and Miles are fixing up a bike for a race. But why won't
Miles tell Tomas where he lives or invite him over?

Art Director: Heather Kindseth
Graphic Designer: Brann Garvey

1 2 3 4 5 6 13 12 11 10 09 08

Printed in the United States of America

TABLE OF CONTENTS

#

The bus started to pull away from the curb. "Wait!" I yelled. I was only a block away. "Wait for me!"

The driver didn't hear me. The bus kept going.

I ran after it for a couple of minutes, but there was no point. It wasn't stopping.

That wasn't good. I was late for school. Again.

I stopped next to a telephone pole to catch my breath. That's when I saw the sign. "Bike race this Saturday," the bright green piece of paper said.

Cool! I thought.

I leaned closer. The ad said that the bike race was to raise money for the Stone Brook Homeless Shelter.

My mom and I went there on Thanksgiving one year. We helped serve a Thanksgiving dinner to all the people who lived there.

I had been surprised by the people. Some of them wore old, worn-out clothes. But some of them just looked like anybody, like they could have been my neighbors or my teachers or my friends.

I looked back at the ad. To enter the race, all you had to do was collect donations. It said you could bring canned food or old clothes or anything that would help the shelter.

The winner would get their picture in the paper, but I didn't care about that. All I cared about was that I had a great shot at winning that race.

I was the fastest runner in my class for sure. I was also one of the strongest swimmers. I loved pushing myself. The bike race would be a perfect way to do that.

There was only one problem. I didn't have a bike.

Chapter 2

Just then, I looked up. There was a kid walking down the street. He looked like he was about thirteen, like me. He was pulling a rusty bike behind him.

The guy walked up to a big Dumpster and lifted the bike up. He was going to throw it away! I couldn't believe my good luck.

"Stop!" I yelled. "Don't throw that bike away. I need it!"

I ran over to the kid. "Don't throw that away," I repeated.

"Why not?" he asked. "It's old and rusty. It doesn't even work anymore."

"Maybe I can fix it up," I told him. "Or we both could, or something. I want to ride it in the bike race this weekend."

The guy looked down at the ground. "The one for Stone Brook?" he asked.

"Yeah," I said. "I want to ride in the race, but I don't have a bike, and I don't have time to save up to buy one. I'm Tomas, by the way."

The guy smiled. He looked kind of nervous. "I'm Miles," he told me. I smiled at him. Then Miles asked, "Why do you want to ride in the race?"

I thought about it for a second. "I think it would be really fun," I told him. "Besides, it's for a good cause. If I get a lot of donations, it will help the people who live at Stone Brook."

Miles frowned. He didn't seem to like the idea. So I added, "Plus, we could get our picture in the paper!"

"Our picture?" Miles asked. "I thought you said you were the one who was going to ride in the race."

"I am," I said. "But if you help me, we can be a team. Maybe we can even enter the race as a team. One of us will ride the bike, and the other one will be the pit crew. Like in NASCAR!"

"Well, okay," Miles said. "There's just one problem."

"What?" I asked.

Miles sighed. "We have to fix up this piece of junk first," he said, pointing to the bike.

I looked at the bike. The tires were flat. The chain was rusted. One of the lines to the brakes was cut. And the handlebars looked like they'd been put on crooked.

"You're not kidding," I told Miles. "We better get started soon!"

Chapter 3

DEEP, DARK SECRETS

The next day after school, Miles met me in my garage. The first thing we did was try to inflate the tires. Luckily, they held the air. That meant there weren't any holes in them.

"Maybe it's our lucky day," I said.

Then we tried to get the chain off the bike. I had stopped at the bike store on my way home to pick up a few supplies.

One of the things I had bought was a new chain. But the old one wouldn't come off.

"Pull harder!" Miles said.

"I am pulling!" I said back.

We pulled as hard as we could. Finally, it came off. But it came off in three pieces.

We kept working. After a while, we needed a break. I went inside and got a couple glasses of juice. I handed one to Miles.

He said, "Thanks." Then he paused. "Why are you so excited to ride in this race?" he asked me.

"I don't know," I said, shrugging. "I guess I thought it would be fun. And it will help all those poor people who live in the homeless shelter. My mom says that people who live there don't have jobs or families or anywhere to stay."

Miles got an angry look on his face. "A lot of them have families," he said. "They have jobs, too. Just because they're poor doesn't mean they don't have other things. You shouldn't judge people."

"Sorry," I said. "I didn't mean to judge anybody. I just want to help them out. Why do you care so much?"

Miles shook his head. "Let's just drop it," he said. "Okay?"

"Fine," I said. I picked up a wrench to start trying to remove the handlebars.

We didn't talk for a few minutes. I was starting to feel uncomfortable. I tried to think of something to say to Miles. Finally, I said, "Let's play a game. Tell me something you never told anybody else before."

Miles looked shocked. "That sounds like a game girls play at sleepovers," he said.

I laughed. "Yeah, I guess it kind of does," I said. "I'll go first."

Miles nodded.

I thought for a few seconds. Then I laughed. "When I was seven, I thought that my teacher was really a werewolf," I told him.

Miles laughed too. "What? Why?" he asked.

"She had this hair that grew out of a mole on her upper lip," I explained. "I really thought she was a werewolf. I was so scared of her. I didn't tell anyone. I was afraid she'd find out."

Miles was laughing so hard. I started to feel embarrassed. "It's not that funny!" I said.

"Yeah, it is," Miles said.

"I thought she'd eat me!" I yelled.

Miles kept laughing. Finally, I laughed too. "Okay, your turn," I said. "Got any deep, dark secrets?"

Miles thought for a few seconds. "Well, sometimes I have this dream where my mom and my sister and I are playing a board game in a living room," he said.

I waited for him to keep going, but he didn't say anything else.

"That's it?" I asked. "I don't get it. How is that a big secret?"

Miles's face turned red. "Never mind," he said. "I have to go."

Then he got up and took off.

"Bye," I said to the empty garage.

Chapter 4

THE CHEETAHS

Miles came back the next day after school. Soon, we were almost done with the bike. All we had to do was attach some reflectors to the back.

I opened up the pack of reflectors. They would be attached to the bike with bolts.

Miles used a wrench to tighten the bolts. Then we stood up and looked at the bike.

"I can't believe we did it!" I said. "We have a bike that's ready to win!"

Miles smiled. "We need a team name," he said.

We thought about it for a while. "Team Panther?" Miles suggested.

"Nah," I said. "How about the Grease Monkeys?"

"I don't know," Miles said. Then he smiled and said, "I got it! How about the Cheetahs? They're fast, they're cool, and since we're kind of bending the rules by being a team, it's funny!"

"I don't get it," I said.

"Cheetahs!" Miles shouted. "Like cheaters!"

"Perfect!" I said, laughing. "Come on, let's see how this thing rides!"

We brought the bike out to the driveway. Then we took turns riding it. The bike rode like a dream.

Finally, it started getting dark. "I should go," Miles said.

"I could walk with you," I suggested. "We could take turns riding the bike on the way. Then I could ride it home."

Miles frowned. He looked mad again. "No, that's okay," he muttered. "I have to go." Then he started walking away, fast.

"Miles, wait!" I called after him. But Miles just kept going.

I didn't want to follow him, but I felt like I had to. So after he turned the corner, I took off after him. He didn't look back. He didn't know I was there.

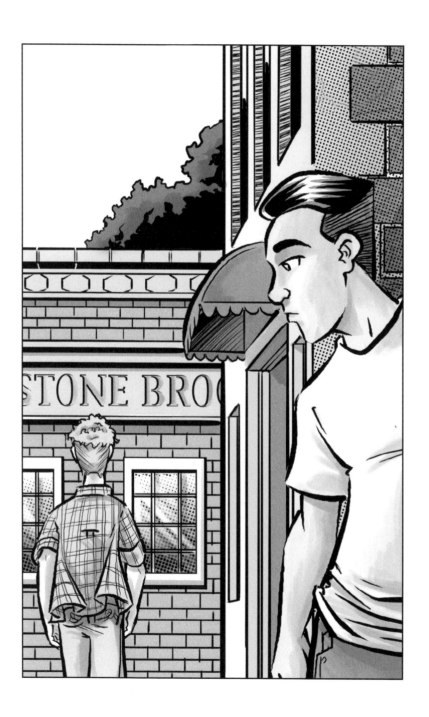

I followed Miles all the way to Stone Brook Homeless Shelter. When he went inside, I went up to the window. I saw a woman walk over to Miles. She gave him a hug.

The woman had red hair, just like Miles did.

"That's his mom!" I whispered.

Chapter 5

The next day was the day of the big race. I rode the bike to the park where the race started.

A lot of people were there. I noticed that there was a TV camera there, and there were some newspaper reporters too. But I didn't see Miles.

What if he saw me last night? I thought. *Would he be too embarrassed to come today?*

Just as I was about to give up, someone grabbed my arm. I turned around. It was Miles.

"Hi, Tomas!" Miles said.

"Hey, Miles," I said. I was nervous, so I just started talking. "I didn't think you were going to make it, after I found out where you—"

I stopped talking, but it was too late.

"Where I what?" Miles asked quietly.

I sighed. "Where you live," I said.

"How did you find out?" he asked.

"I followed you," I admitted. "I saw you go into the shelter."

Miles looked down at his shoes. "Yeah," he said. "I live at Stone Brook."

"Why didn't you say anything?" I asked.

Miles shrugged. "I don't know," he said. "It's not that I'm embarrassed. It's just that your house was so nice, and stuff. Right now, my mom doesn't have a job. My dad died a couple of years ago. I guess I didn't tell you because I just wanted to pretend like I was normal."

He took a deep breath. Then he said, "We don't have to be friends anymore if you don't want to."

I was shocked. "What?" I said. "That's crazy! Of course I still want to be friends. Why wouldn't I?"

"I don't know," Miles said. "I guess I figured you wouldn't want to because I don't have a garage we can work in or a house we can watch TV in or anything."

"Who cares?" I asked. "It's cool. Besides, if it wasn't for you, we never would've had this cool bike," I added.

"Right," he said.

Just then, a voice said, "It's time for the race to begin! Everyone to the starting line."

"Tell you what," I said. "If you let me be the one to ride in the race, you can keep the bike."

"I don't have a place to keep it," Miles said quietly.

"Yeah you do," I told him. "You can keep it in my garage, until your family has a garage too."

Miles gave me a high five. "Sounds like a plan," he said.

Then I rode Miles's bike to the starting line.

ABOUT THE AUTHOR

Jon Mikkelsen has written dozens of plays for kids, which have involved aliens, superheroes, and more aliens. He acts on stage and loves performing in front of an audience. Jon also loves sushi, cheeseburgers, and pizza. He loves to travel, and has visited Moscow, Berlin, London, and Amsterdam. He lives in Minneapolis and has a cat named Coco, who does not pay rent.

ABOUT THE ILLUSTRATOR

Nathan Lueth has been a freelance illustrator since 2004. He graduated from the Minneapolis College of Art and Design in 2004, and has done work for companies like Target, General Mills, and Wreked Records. Nathan was a 2008 finalist in Tokyopop's Rising Stars of Manga contest. He lives in Minneapolis, Minnesota.

GLOSSARY

crooked (KRUK-id)—not going in a straight line

curb (KURB)—the raised border along the edge of a paved street

donations (doh-NAY-shuhnz)—something given for free, usually to help someone else

embarrassed (em-BAIR-uhssd)—if you are embarrassed, you feel awkward and uncomfortable

handlebars (HAN-duhl-barz)—the bar at the front of a bicycle or motorcycle that you use for steering

inflate (in-FLATE)—to make something expand by blowing or pumping air into it

judge (JUHJ)—to form an opinion about someone or something

reflectors (ri-FLEK-turz)—shiny devices that bounce back light

shelter (SHEL-tur)—a place where a homeless person or victim of a disaster can stay

wrench (RENCH)—a tool with jaws for tightening and loosening bolts

DISCUSSION QUESTIONS

1. Tomas follows Miles to the homeless shelter. Do you think that was the right thing to do? Why or why not?

2. The team name that Miles and Tomas come up with is the Cheetahs. Can you think of any other names that would work for their team?

3. Do you think Miles and Tomas will continue to be friends after the bike race? Why or why not?

WRITING PROMPTS

1. At the end of this book, Tomas is getting ready to race. What do you think happens next?

2. Tomas's secret is that he once thought his teacher was a werewolf. Miles's is that he wishes his family had a home. What is one of your secrets?

3. Miles and Tomas work together to fix up the bike. What is something that you do with your friends? Write about it.

MORE ABOUT HOMELESSNESS

Every year, there are 3.5 million homeless people in the United States. More than 1 million of them are children. That means that about one of every 100 people in the United States is homeless. Some of those people are families; others are single men or women.

It used to be thought that only criminals and mentally ill people were homeless. Now, we know that homelessness can affect anyone.

Some people are homeless for only a week or so. Others can be homeless for years. Even people who have jobs during the day may be homeless at night.

Some homeless people stay in homeless shelters.

A shelter is a place where homeless people can sleep and sometimes eat meals. Usually, the shelter requires the people to leave during the day.

In some places, there are daytime shelters. These are open when regular nighttime shelters aren't, so that people have a safe place to stay during the day.

Lots of homeless kids go to school. They are regular kids, just like everyone else. There isn't anything different about them except the place where they sleep.

INTERNET SITES

Do you want to know more about subjects related to this book? Or are you interested in learning about other topics? Then check out FactHound, a fun, easy way to find Internet sites.

Our investigative staff has already sniffed out great sites for you!

Here's how to use FactHound:

1. Visit *www.facthound.com*

2. Select your grade level.

3. To learn more about subjects related to this book, type in the book's ISBN number: **9781434207869**.

4. Click the **Fetch It** button.

FactHound will fetch the best Internet sites for you!